Park Stories: *Kensington Gardens*

Park Stories: A Beauty Parlour for Swans
© Hanan al-Shaykh 2009

ISBN: 978-0-9558761-4-1

Series Editor: Rowan Routh

Published by The Royal Parks
www.royalparks.org.uk

Production by Strange Attractor Press
BM SAP, London, WC1N 3XX, UK
www.strangeattractor.co.uk

Cover design: Ali Hutchinson

Park Stories devised by Rowan Routh

The Royal Parks gratefully acknowledges the financial support of Arts Council England.

Printed by Kennet Print, Devizes, UK on 100% post-consumer recycled Cyclus offset paper using vegetable-based inks.

A Beauty Parlour for Swans

Hanan al-Shaykh

THE
**ROYAL
PARKS**

A Beauty Parlour for Swans

At last I entered Kensington Gardens. I'd been wanting to go there for weeks, but I'd been afraid to trick my mother and brother into letting me out of the flat alone. I was worried my brother would catch me and that I would stutter when I spoke to the boy and he would notice how my right temple throbbed and how shy I was in front of men.

In the blink of an eye I was through the gates, which I had often gazed down at from the window of the flat. But instead of breathing a sigh of relief, I panicked. Kensington Gardens was an endless green desert. The paths, which I'd thought I knew like the back of my hand, stretched out before me like a tangle of coloured thread.

I hurried back out through the same gate and kept going until our building came into view. I looked up to the ninth floor and saw the net curtains. I pictured my mother sitting with my father, who was recovering from his recent heart operation. Reassured, I swiftly made my way back into the park, mindful of the day's miracle. It had begun when my brother decided to go to a football match with a friend from our neighbourhood back in Kuwait. My mother was angry with him for failing to take me to the laundrette yet again, without a thought for the washing, which was piled up like the Pyramids. So she'd let me go by myself, since it was just round the corner. The miracle did not stop there though, for the boy who'd been phoning me every day, urging me to meet him, said he would drop everything if I told him I had the opportunity to leave the flat alone. We arranged a time to meet in Kensington Gardens. 'By the Diana, Princess of Wales Memorial Playground,' he'd said.

I hurried to the laundrette and handed the washing

to the attendant. For a moment I felt bad deceiving my
mother. I'd been so delighted when she gave me permission
to go out that, fearing she'd grow suspicious, I'd lied about
how much I'd longed for this little adventure – to be able
to follow the instructions on the washing machine and
dryer and perform the task myself. She refused to send our
clothes to the dry-cleaner – she wanted to save as much as
possible of what the Kuwaiti Embassy had given us for living
expenses while in London, 'in addition to bearing the cost of
the operation and air tickets'.

    Back in Kensington Gardens, I stepped on to the
green grass. I imagined I was treading on chickpeas. I used
to wrap chickpeas in cotton and soak them in water for a
day until green shoots sprouted, just as our Iranian science
teacher had shown us. The grass beneath me was a soft
carpet. I stepped back onto the path.

    I saw a daisy, tiny, like a grain of white sugar. I
leaned down and picked it, with its soft velvety fuzz and
beautiful white crown reminding me of a bride's tiara. I'd
never before dared to meet a boy. It seemed possible only
because I was in London. In Kuwait I'd had to make do
with exchanging looks and text messages and the occasional
phone call. Kuwait was a small city and everyone knew
each other. They were like columns of ants that stopped in
greeting before marching on.

    I'd never heard of Kensington Gardens. I had
thought there was only one park in London, called 'Hyde
Park' because people could hide there, a place where lovers
met. A friend told me how she'd arranged to meet a boy
from Kuwait in Hyde Park last year, on a visit to London.
I shuddered with fear as she recounted how they'd walked
together and how she'd let him hold her hand. He'd even
planted a kiss on her cheek. Where was the Diana, Princess
of Wales Memorial Playground?

    All I could see around me were open spaces and

green trees. I was glad I still had an hour to find the playground.
I'd discovered that in London finding your way around, not
the language, was the first obstacle for visitors. English places
were strange to the Arab eye in every way, even their stone
and architecture. Everyone I might have asked for directions
was in a hurry. I envied a dog that ran past confidently. Finally,
I summoned the courage to ask a woman who was strolling
along, but she apologised; she didn't know the park either.
She pointed to a cluster of signs. As I drew near I saw an
arrow pointing to the playground. I walked on, accompanied
by birds cheeping as they moved from the trees to the sky to
the grass. One was black and white like a penguin. Another
was grey, the size of an eagle, and stood on one leg as still as
a statue. Was it a statue? I turned to look again and suddenly
it came to life, grabbing a dead mouse in its beak and spinning
it like a merry-go-round.

An old man threw red peanuts to a squirrel. It held
one in both hands, like a child eating a sandwich. Three
pigeons pinched the rest of the nuts and chased the squirrel
away when it neared.

I reached some tall trees with birds' nests high in
the branches. Where did birds build their nests in Kuwait,
I wondered. How come I'd never seen a single nest in
my nineteen years? I stopped by a large cone-shaped tree
completely covered in leaves and pulled back its branches
as though I was drawing a curtain. I saw its heart, its trunk,
wrapped in dry twigs like barbed wire. It resembled a
woman wrapped in an *abaya* from head to toe, like me,
except today I was wearing a dark blue coat, long pink skirt
and embroidered headscarf. I'd convinced my brother and
mother to let me go out without my *abaya* after the spitting
incident. The Englishman had looked at my mother and
I with such contempt as we waited for a taxi outside the
hospital, and when our eyes met he had spat on the ground.

In Kuwait I was like this tree. Inside me was a dark,

wilful world that bore no relation to the image I projected to my family of an optimistic young girl content with tradition despite its restrictions. I obeyed my family, even when they forbade simple pleasures like going out with friends to restaurants, or going out with my mother without an *abaya*.

My heart jumped suddenly. What if my brother decided not to go to the match? What if the match only lasted half an hour and he couldn't find me amid the roar of washing machines and dryers?

I saw a blue circle in the distance. White shapes moved, then froze. I approached a pond with large ducks, which I knew were called swans, on its banks. Each one was doing its own thing. One raised its wings and fluttered them like aeroplane propellers. Another stood on one leg, a third pecked at its white feathers. It was like a beauty parlour for swans. I could see more than twenty-five of them with their orange beaks emphasising their black eyes, which, along with their thick eyebrows, looked as though they'd been lined with kohl. I hovered, watching them, unable to tear myself away. Then the sun appeared, casting its light on the water, and I realised I'd lost my bearings. I wanted to ask for directions from a woman and her young son who were standing in front of a tree trunk encased in a large cage, but they were engrossed. They laughed and pointed, their faces filled with happiness. As I drew close I saw elves and animals hidden, or rather carved, in the folds of the trunk. I recognised the owl, squirrel, rabbit, crow and other creatures. I found myself staring at the figure of a girl carved in the trunk. She was wearing a red flowing dress, her long hair hung loose. She looked completely at ease, unbothered by the elves encircling her. I wondered who she was. Why did I envy her when she was no bigger than a hand and carved in a tree trunk, a prisoner in a cage? I turned and marched on down the main pathway.

'Where is the Diana, Princess of Wales Memorial Playground?' I eventually asked a woman pushing her child in a pram. She suggested I walk with her. A van was passing slowly and we made way for it. The driver stuck his head out of the window. 'Thanks darling.' I was pleased to be called darling here, just as I'd been pleased to be called darling by the Lebanese boy. I'd watched the boy from morning to evening for ten days at the hospital. His sister had been in a car accident, and with exemplary patience and kindness he was teaching her to walk again. I had watched him comfort her and rub her hair and dry her tears. My heart raced when our eyes met. When he asked for my number, I decided to embroider it in white on my dark headscarf. If he noticed and telephoned I would talk to him. If he didn't, I'd know it wasn't to be.

I sat in front of him in the visitors' room the next day with my headscarf spread over my shoulders. He phoned a few minutes later and thanked me. That afternoon he sent me a text, asking if he could see me alone away from the hospital.

'We're here. This is the playground,' said the woman. I was surprised to find myself a few steps away from the tree with the elves and the lady in the red dress. I smiled at her and stood at the entrance to wait for the Lebanese boy. How could I have missed the playground? I had a quarter of an hour to go. But I didn't wait. Something made me run to the pond and raise my arms, fluttering them like the swans. I jumped in the air like the birds. I seized my heart in my hands, like the squirrel with the red peanut. I was that squirrel. I was that daisy craning its neck in the grass.

'Well done,' my heart cried. I saw a group of green parrots flying from tree to tree. Some people had stopped to watch them. 'No doubt they've escaped from a cage in someone's house,' I heard a man say. I had escaped like the parrots. I couldn't keep up with my feet. I ran without tiring.

I ran for the first time since I'd stopped running years ago, when they told me it wasn't suitable because I was a girl. I was running now on my own, thinking on my own. I caught up with my legs and recovered them. I recovered my face, my chest, my waist, my hips, my fingers. I recovered my whole self. I turned in a circle and tore off my family like a heavy coat.

I left the cone-shaped tree and ran to another with outstretched branches and hugged it. I said goodbye to the Sara who for two weeks had been afraid to look out the window onto the park lest her family guessed that she would one day enter it alone.

I looked up to the ninth floor where my mother sat all day long in the rented flat, not daring to cross the threshold and take the lift. But I was no longer reassured by the thought of its curtains wrapped around me.

A fresh gust blew in my direction and I inhaled. It lingered and brought with it everyone from the park to give me strength... the swans, the birds, the lone daisy, the elf-woman in her red dress... And the Lebanese boy? I could see him another time!

Translated by Christina Phillips

أودع سارة التي ولدة أسبوعين خافت أن تسترق النظر من النافذة إلى كانزنكتون غاردنز، خائفة من ان تحزر عائلتها أنها ستدخلها ذات يوم وحيدة.

أرفع نظري إلى أعلى حيث الطابق التاسع، حيث أمي تجلس ليل نهار، في هذه الشقة المفروشة ولا تتجرأ حتى على الخطو خطوة واحدة عبر العتبة واخذ المصعد وحيدة.

رؤيتي للستارة إياها في الطابق التاسع لا تطمئنني هذه المرة.

لكن الهواء الشهي يسرع إلي فأتنفسه، ولا يتركني بل يصطحب معه كل من في الكانزنكتون غاردنز لنجدتي.. البجع. زقزقة العصافير والاقحوانه الوحيدة والجنية ذات الرداء الأحمر.. والشاب اللبناني؟

لا بأس سأراه مرة أخرى!

انعطفت أسير وأسير على ممر رئيسي " أين ملعب الأميرة ديانا من فضلك" سألت امرأة كانت تجر طفلها في عربة، اقترحت علي أن تسير معي لأنها كانت تقصد الملعب، إنها تعود بي باتجاه البحيرة المستديرة إياها، لا بد أني لحقت السهم الخطأ. استوقفتنا سيارة تسير الهويناء عندما أفسحنا لها الطريق، مد السائق وجهه وخاطبني: شكرا يا حبيبتي، فرحت لتسميته لي بالحبيبة كما فرحت بمناداة بالشاب اللبناني لي بالحبيبة بعد أن دأبت على رؤيته في النهار وفي الساعات الأولى من المغرب طيلة عشرة أيام في المستشفى. كان الشاب يزور أخته التي أصيبت بحادث سيارة، وراح يعلمها بكل صبر وحنان كيفية السير من جديد.. راقبته وهو يواسبها، وهو يمسد لها شعرها ويجفف لها دموعها. التقت نظراتنا وأسرعت إليه دقات قلبي وحطت على وجهه. وبدلا من إعطائه رقم هاتفي النقال الذي طلب مني مرات عدة، قمت بتطريزه بالخيط الأبيض على لفحة رأسي الغامقة اللون، مشترطة على نفسي، إذا انتبه إلى ما فعلته واتصل بي سأرحب به وأحادثه، أما إذا لم ينتبه فسأقتنع بأنه لا نصيب بيننا.
جلست أمامه في اليوم التالي في غرفة استقبال زوار المرضى، عرضت لفحة رأسي المتدلية فوق كتفي، اتصل بي بعد لحظات يشكرني على منح رقمي النقال. في عصر اليوم نفسه أرسل لي رسالة على نقالي يطلب مني رؤيتي وحيدين خارج المستشفى.

" وصلنا، ها هو الملعب " قالت لي المرأة، ابتسمت لها تعجبت وأنا أجد نفسي على بعد خطوات من الشجرة ،حيث الاقزام والجنية ذات الرداء الاحمر، ابتسمت لها. وقفت على مدخله انتظر الشاب اللبناني.كيف حدث بأني لم ار ملعب ديانا ؟ بقي ربع ساعة على موعدي، لم انتظر، حركة خارجة عن إرادتي جعلتني أسرع إلى حيث البحيرة، رفعت ذراعي ورفرفت بهما تماما كالبجع، قفزت في الهواء كما تقفز الطيور، أمسكت بقلبي بين يدي، كما امسك السنجاب بحبة الفستق الحمراء، أنا هذا السنجاب. أنا الاقحوانه إياها التي اشرأبت برأسها وحيدة بين العشب الأخضر.
"حسنا فعلت" هتف قلبي وأكثر من ببغاء أخضر يطير من شجرة إلى أخرى أمام مجموعة من الناس وقفوا يلاحقونها بأعينهم، نسمع رجلا يعلق" لا بد أنها هربت من قفص في بيت خاص بها".
هربت وركضت كالببغاءات . لا استطيع اللحاق بقدمي، ركضت من غير تعب او ملل، ركضت كأني أركض لاول مرة منذ أن توقفت عن الركض، عندما قيل لي بأني بنت. أركض ألان وحدي، وأفكر وحدي، ألحق بساقي وأسترجعهما، أسترجع وجهي وصدري وخصري ووركي وأناملي. استرجع كلي.. وأدور حول نفسي سعيدة، أخلع عني عائلتي وكأنها معطف ثقيل.
اترك الشجرة الشبيبة بكوز الصنوبر واركض إلى الشجرة التي تفرد أغصانها وأضمها إلي.

5

بتغطيتها من قمة رأسها حتى أخمص قدميها. أجدني أزيح أغصانها وكأني أزيح ستارة، فأرى قلبها، جذعها وقد التف حوله الأغصان الجافة وكأنها أسلاك شائكة، هذه الشجرة تشبه أمرأة تلتف بالعباءة من رأسها تلامس الأرض. تشبهني بنفسي. رغم أني ألان أسير بمعطف كحلي اللون، وتنوره طويلة زهرية اللون، ولفحة رأسي المزركشة. أقنعت أخي وأمي بالسماح لي بعدم ارتداء العباءة ما دمت في لندن ، اثر تلك البصقة.

رجل انكليزي نظر إلي وألى أمي نظرة عداوة ونحن ننتظر تاكسيا قرب المستشفى ،وحين التقت عيناه بعيني، حتى بصق على الأرض.

في الكويت أبدو كهذه الشجرة، داخلي سري، عنيد، مظلم لا يطابق الصورة التي اعكسها أمام عائلتي والآخرين متظاهرة بأني شابة متفائلة، راضية بالتقاليد ولو أنها متزمتة، وبأني أطيع كل ما يشار به علي.بكل صبر حتى ولو حرمت من متع بسيطة، كالذهاب وحيدة مع صديقاتي إلى مطعم، والسير مع أمي من غير عباءة.

يهارشني قلبي فجأة ، ماذا لو بدل أخي رأيه ولم يذهب إلى ماتش الكرة ؟ ماذا لو انتهى الماتش خلال نصف ساعة وجاء إلى المغسلة ولم يجدني بين هدير الغسالات والنشافات.

دائرة زرقاء، رأيتها عن بعد. أشباح بيضاء جمدت ثم تحركت تعرفني بأنه يدعى بالبجع، اقتربت من بحيرة على ضفافها البط الكبير الذي فطنت بأنه يدعى بالبجع، كل واحدة منها قامت بحركة مختلفة عن الأخرى، رفعت احدها جناحيها فرفرفت بهما كأنهما مروحتا طائرة، بينما وقفت أخرى على قدم واحدة، ودفنت ثالثة رأسها تنقد ريشها الأبيض. ترى هل أنا في صالون للتجميل خاص بالبجع؟

أكثر من خمسة وعشرين بجعة صبغت مناقيرها باللون البرتقالي لا الأحمر من أجل أن تسلط الأضواء على أعينها المكحلة بالكحل الأسود، وعلى حواجبها السميكة، لحقت بها مفتونة لا اقوى على مفارقتها. الشمس بزغت فجأة وطرحت نفسها فوق الماء. أتبين بأني قد أضعت طريقي. أحاول أن أسأل من جديد امرأة وقفت مع صغيرها أمام قفص كبير بداخله جذع شجرة، لكنها انشغلت عني مع صغيرها وهما يضحكان ويشيران بالأصابع والفرح باد على وجه كل منهما. وحين حشرت نفسي قربهما، تبينت تماثيل أقزام وجن، حيوانات مختبئة بل محفورة بين طيات هذا الجذع من الشجرة ، ولم أتعرف إلا على البومة والسنجاب والأرنب والغراب من بين عشرات الحيوانات والكائنات. ثمة امرأة بينها أسدلت شعرها الطويل وتمددت بردائها الأحمر، بدت سعيدة كل السعادة غير خائفة من الأقزام والجن حولها، من تكون هذه المرأة ؟ لماذا أغبطها؟ لأنها أكثر حظا مني رغم أن حجمها لا يتعدى حجم الكف، كما أنها محفورة على جذع شجرة، رهينة هذا القفص؟

لتشب منها النبتة الخضراء، كما أشارت علينا مدرسة العلوم الإيرانية، العشب تحت قدمي سجادة وثيرة، لكني حدت عنه.

رأيت زهرة من الأقحوان ، تشبه حبة سكر بيضاء ، انحنيت اقطف الاقحوانة الحقيقية.فقد الزغب الأصفر المخملي والتاج الأبيض الجميل الذي يشبه تاج إكليل العروس. هذه هي المرة الأولى التي أتجرأ فيها وأوافق على لقاء شاب. طبعا لأني في لندن.

أما في الكويت فأنا أكتفي بتبادل النظرات ورسائل النقال، لأسمح لنفسي بين الحين والحين بالتحدث في التلفون، فالكويت بالتالي مدينة صغيرة والناس تعرف بعضها فتراهم في الشوارع يتوقفون ويتصافحون فيبدون كصف النمل.

لم أكن سمعت بكازنزكتون غاردنز من قبل ، ظننت أن هناك بارك واحد في لندن يدعى " هايد بارك" اسم على مسمى يدخله المرء ليختبئ به "هايد" أنه المكان للقاء الأحبة.فقد أخبرتني صديقة لي زارت لندن في العام الماضي مع أهلها، بأنها تواعدت مع الشاب الذي أحبته في الكويت على اللقاء به في الهايد بارك، كيف مشيا معا وكيف دعته يمسك بيدها.. بل وأن يمنحها قبلة سريعة على الخد.. ترى أين هو ملعب الأميرة ديانا؟؟؟

لا أرى سوى مساحات وأشجار خضراء على امتداد البصر. أهنيء نفسي لأنه ما زال عندي ساعة على موعد اللقاء كي استدل على الملعب. اكتشفت وأنا في لندن أن المكان هو العائق الأول للزائرين قبل اللغة.الأمكنة الانكليزية ، هي غريبة كل الغرابة على الأعين العربية في كل شيء حتى في حجارتها وهندستها ، كل من صادفته حتى ألان من اجل أن استدله على الطريق كان على عجلة من أمره. تملكت الشجاعة وسألت امرأة تسير الهوينا ، فاعتذرت لانها غريبة مثلي ، وأشارت باتجاه عامود اعتله عدة يافطات .أول ما رأيت حين وصلت إليه سهما يشير إلى ملعب الأميرة ديانا.

مضيت، ترافقني زقزقة ونداء العصافير والطيور وهي تتقافز من الأشجار الى الفضاء إلى العشب، طائر أسود وأبيض كأنه البطريق وهناك طائر رمادي اللون بحجم النسر، وقف على قدم واحدة لا يتحرك كأنه التمثال، لا بل أنه تمثال التفت إلى الخلف لأنظر إليه نظرة أخيرة، وإذا بالروح قد دبت فيه فجأة، أمسك بمنقاره فأرة ميتة وأخذ يلوح بها بحركة دائرية وكأنها "دويخه".

رجل مسن رمى لسنجاب الفستق الأحمر، أمسكها بكلتا يديه كطفل يأكل ساندويتش، ثلاثة حمامات تستولي على باقي الفستق، وتطرد السنجاب حين اقترب منها.

وصلت إلى الأشجار الباسقة ، والأعشاش بين أغصانها. ترى أين تبني العصافير أعشاشها في الكويت ؟ وكيف اتفق أنني لم أر ولو عشا واحدا في حياتي، رغم سنواتي التسع عشرة ؟ أقف أمام شجرة تشبه كوز الصنوبر ، قامت أوراقها

صالون تجميل للبجع

أخيرا ، بعد تردد دام أكثر من أسبوعين، دخلت كانزنكتون غاردنز ،كنت خائفة من التحايل على أمي وأخي من أجل أن أغادر الشقة بمفردي وألتقي بالشاب. كنت خائفة أن يضبطني أخي معه، و خائفة أيضا أن أتلعثم وأنا أتحدث مع الشاب فيلاحظ كيف ينبض صدغي من الجهة اليمنى خجلا كلما تحدثت إلى رجل. وبلمح البصر دخلت بوابتها المفتوحة، التي طالما راقبتها من نافذة شقتنا المستأجرة، وبدلا من أن أتنفس الصعداء وجدتني أرتعد خوفا . كانزنكتون غاردنز ما هي إلا صحراء خضراء، لا بداية لها ولا نهاية، دروبها التي أيقنت أني حفظتها ككف يدي، امتدت أمامي الان وكأنها خيوط ملونة تشابكت واختلطت..

أسرعت بالخروج من غير تردد من البوابة إياها إلى أن تبينت البناية التي نــكنها، نـظرت سني إلى الطابق التاسع وروبني للساره الحفيهه إياها وتخيلي أمي جالسة قرب والدي الذي كان يتعافى من جراء عملية القلب التي أجريت له هنا قبل أسبوعين جعلتني اشعر بالطمأنينة، لذلك عدت ادخل كانزكتون غاردنز من جديد..

لن أضيع المعجزة التي حدثت من اجلي هذا اليوم ابتداء من أخي الذي قرر أن يحضر ماتش كرة بعدأن اتصل به صديق له كويتي (من ديرتنا)، وهو ما أغضب أمي منه لأنه أرجا من جديد اصطحابي إلى المغسلة العمومية، غير مبال بالغسيل التي تكدس كالاهرامات مما أدى، إلى سماح أمي لي مكرهه بالذهاب بمفردي إلى المغسلة... التي كانت قريبة جدا، ولم تتوقف المعجزة عند هذا الحد بل أنها تدخلت وجعلت الشاب الذي كان يتصل بي عبر الهاتف النقال كل يوم ويحثني على لقائه يهتف ألان مؤكدًا بأنه يترك كل شيء ويسرع لرؤيتي، فاتفقنا على موعد، في كانزنكتون غاردنز، و" عند ملعب الأميرة ديانا".

أسرعت إلى المغسلة اسلم الغسيل إلى المسئولة هناك ولسة من الحزن تمر على قلبي، لتحايلي على أمي.فانا قد صفقت فرحا ما أن سمحت لي والدتي بالخروج، لكني خوفا من شكوكها أضفت لأسباب سعادتي أضفت كاذبة بأني أتوق لهذه المغامرة في الغسيل وإتباع تعليمات الغسالة والنشافة وانجاز المهمة بنفسي، وكانت أمي قد أبت أن نرسل غسيلنا إلى المصبغة من اجل أن توفر قدر المستطاع ما كانت السفارة الكويتية تمنحه لنا أسبوعيا كمصروف لإقامتنا في لندن " إلى جانب تكبد السفارة مصاريف العملية الجراحية وتذاكر السفر".

أسيروأنا في كانزنكتون غاردنز من جديد فوق العشب الأخضر، وكأني أسير فوق ملايين من حبوب الحمص.. كنت أغمس الحبيبات في القطن وأبله بالماء كل يوم،

2

صالون تجميل للبجع

حنان الشيخ

THE
ROYAL
PARKS